50

# OBSOLETE MATERIALS

© Copyright 1971 by Gakken Co., Ltd.
Published by Gakken Co., Ltd., Tokyo, Japan
First Japanese Publication, 1968
Distributed in the United States by
Silver Burdett Company, Morristown, New Jersey 07960
Library of Congress Catalog Card Number: 77-94809
Printed and bound in Japan

Sergey S. Prokofiev's

# PETER AND THE WOLF

782.1

retold by Ann King Herring
illustrated by Kozo Shimizu
photographed by Yasuji Yajima

Fantasia Pictorial
Stories from Famous Music

**Gakken**

Early one bright spring morning, Peter went outside, all by himself, and opened the garden gate. His friend the bird was sitting in a tree by the wall.

"Good morning, Peter," trilled the bird.

"Good morning," Peter answered. "I am going out into the meadow. Won't you come?"

Soon a duck came waddling around to the gate. She was delighted when she found it open, because now she could go for a morning swim on the pond in the meadow.

When the little bird saw the duck paddling, he flew around and around the pond, teasing her.

"You are not much of a bird, are you? Just look at you! You can't even fly."

But the duck only laughed at him. "I shouldn't talk if I were you!" she quacked. "You call yourself a bird, but just look at you! You can't even swim."

They quarreled and quarreled, but neither one would give in. Just then, Peter noticed something. It was a cat, creeping ever so quietly through the grass.

"I'll catch that bird for my breakfast, be-fore he even knows it," she was thinking.

"Look out!" shouted Peter. The bird flew to safety, high in a tree. The duck quack-ed loudly—from a safe distance out in the middle of the pond.

Just then, Peter's grandfather came out. He was
very, very angry.

"How many times have I told you not to go
into the meadow?" he scolded. "It is more danger-
ous than you can imagine. Tell me now, just what
would you do if a wolf should come out of the
forest?"

Needless to say, Peter was not daunted. He
would not be afraid of a dozen wolves.

But Grandfather had his mind made up. He took Peter's hand, led him back inside the gate . . . and locked it firmly after them.

Just as soon as the gate was locked, Grandpapa's fears came true.

A huge gray wolf bounded out of the forest. The quick-thinking cat clambered up into the tree. The duck quacked louder than ever. She was so frightened that she foolishly jumped out of the water and tried to run.

But her legs were too short. No matter how hard she tried, she could only waddle, and there was no way for her to escape the wolf.

Closer he came and closer. Snap! He caught her, and gulp! In one bite, he swallowed her whole.

So that was all for the duck. And as for the others, you can imagine just how things stood. The cat was standing upon a branch at one side of the tree, while the bird perched on a branch on the other side—as far away as possible from the cat.

On the ground below, the wolf stalked around and around, staring hungrily up at them both.

Meanwhile, Peter stood inside the gate, watching everything that was happening.

Soon he ran into the house. When he came
out again, he was carrying a strong rope.

Then he climbed over the garden wall and
swung himself into the tree.

"Fly down, now, and keep circling around the
wolf's head, just as fast as you can," Peter said to
the bird. "But be careful not to let him catch you!"

Snap! Snap! went the wolf. But the clever bird
was too quick for him.

Peter made a noose in the end of the rope.
Carefully, quickly, he let it down and . . .

. . . with a jerk, he caught the wolf by the tail. How that wolf was surprised! He jumped up, and down, and this way, and that way, trying to free himself.

But Peter had already tied the rope to the tree, and the harder the wolf jumped, the tighter the knot grew.

At that moment, Peter heard a noise of shooting. Some hunters came out of the forest, hot on the wolf's trail.

"Don't shoot!" cried Peter. "Look! We have caught the wolf already, the bird and I. Now, let us take him to the zoo."

Then they all opened their eyes wide with surprise. From somewhere deep inside the wolf, they heard a steady quacking. It was the duck...for, in his haste, the wolf had gulped her down alive.

And so the triumphant procession set off. Peter, of course, marched at the head. After him strode the hunters, leading the wolf.

The little bird perched on Peter's hat, warbling cheerily. "Just see what Peter and I have done!" he sang.

Last of all walked Grandpapa and the cat. "These things are all well and good," muttered Grandpapa, shaking his head grumpily. "This time, it turned out well enough. But what if Peter had NOT caught the wolf? What then?"